AF444081

A MOUTHFUL
OF RIVERS

A MOUTHFUL OF RIVERS

A COLLECTION OF SHORT STORIES AND POEMS

Omale Allen Abdul-Jabbar

Seun Osho

Ayo Oyeku

Nosakhare Collins

Foreword by Dr. Wale Okediran

Published in Nigeria in 2023 by **LIBRETTO Publishers**

LIBRETTO PUBLISHERS LIMITED

HEADOFFICE
No. 1, Lagos Garage, Owode,
Oyo, Oyo State, Nigeria.

BRANCHES
Edo | Abuja
Tel: +234 (0) 807 834 6790, +234 (0) 813 044 6615.
Email: publishing@librettong.com
sales@librettong.com
Website: www.librettong.com
Bookstore Website: www.publishing.librettong.com
Twitter.com/librettopublish | facebook.com/librettong | instagram.com/libretto_ng

ISBN: 978-978-59955-6-5
A catalogue record for this book is available from the National Library of Nigeria.

Cover Design by Seun Osho & Nosakhare Collins
Book Layout & Design & Typesetting by Nosakhare Collins
Printed and Bound in Nigeria by Libretto Publishers Limited

Libretto title is available for bulk purchase for educational and corporate use. Special editions, personalized covers and excerpts from our titles can also be made available at special rates. For more information, contact us at publishing@librettong.com | sales@librettong.com

Praise for A Mouthful Of Rivers

A Mouthful of Rivers is a delightful feast. The unique genesis of this volume, conceived during a literary retreat that brought together its four authors at the Ebedi International Writers Residency, could not be more remarkable. Omale Allen Abdul-Jabar, Seun Osho, Ayo Oyeku and Nosakhare Collins, with commendable imagination and urgency, speak variously to the concerns of our age, yet the synergy of their creative energies makes this book more than the sum of its parts.
—**Rotimi Babatunde,** *Winner of the 2012 Caine Prize.*

Twenty-nine entries of six short stories and twenty-three poems from four brilliant minds is a handful of literary harvest traversing the thematic concerns of birth, death, mental burden, quest for survival, love, nature, the magical and nostalgic among other existential concerns of multiple hue and shade. This is a collection that bears positive testimony to the bright possibilities of the Nigerian literary canvass.
—**Ropo Ewenla,** *Writer, Actor, Broadcaster & Director*

Table of Contents

Section One: Omale Allen Abdul-Jabbar

Section Two: Seun Osho

Foreword

VOICES FROM EBEDI WRITERS RESIDENCY

A FOREWORD to A MOUTHFUL OF RIVERS by Nosakhare Collins, Omale Allen Abdul-Jabbar, Ayo Oyeku and Seun Osho A Collection of Stories and Poems also known to as 'Anthologies' is a good way of bringing together various literary voices in a single publication which can be available to many.

Anthologies are majorly preferred by readers who want to explore different topics, subjects and themes at the same time. They also promote cross-readership and exposure for the contributing authors and for the host organization.

In addition, students and scholars can find anthologies useful for writing academic papers. Although there could be anthologies specific for poetry, short nonfiction articles, essays and reviews, there are also anthologies where these genres can be mixed.

A MOUTHFUL OF RIVERS is the work of four Residents for the August-September 2022 session of the Ebedi International Writers Residency, Iseyin, Nigeria. It is a collection of stories and poems around the experiences of the authors during their stay at the Residency.

The Residency which is a private facility for Writers to work on their Literary works in a conducive environment at no cost, has been in existence since 2010. During this period, it has hosted about 180 writers from 10 different African countries.

In relating their experiences at the Residency, the writers were able to use the book to showcase some of the works undertaken during their stay in the Residency.

In doing this, the writers were able to confirm the relevance of a Writers Residency to the literary careers of writers as aptly reiterated by Dr Nureni Oyewole Fadare, a Senior Lecturer at the Sokoto State University who gave the Keynote Speech at the welcome reception for the first set of the 2023 Fellows at the Residency.

According to Fadare; ''Writers' Residencies are created all over the world to create avenue for creative and academic writers to settle down and complete their on-going works or initiate a new one.

A Writers' Residency is always located in a serene environment such as beside a lake, hill, resort, cottage or castle.

Writing is a private affair and has to be carried out in a conducive atmosphere and environment. In the words of Virginia Woolf, a foremost English feminist writer and author of A Room of One's Own, she said, "…a woman must have money and a room of her own if she is to write fiction."

The argument here is that to have the right state of mind to write, one needs to be independent minded and be physically independent too. Such an atmosphere is created here at Ebedi Writers' residency"

Apart from being a documentation of quality creative works, A MOUTHFUL OF RIVERS is a further affirmation of not only the benefit of a Writers Residency to writers, it is also a testimony to the ability of four Writers to have effectively put to use the facilities offered to them by the Ebedi International Writers Residency.

—Dr. Wale Okediran
Founder, Ebedi International Writers Residency, Iseyin, Nigeria, Secretary General, Pan African Writers Association

Section One

Omale Allen Abdul-Jabbar

Omale Allen Abdul-Jabbar is known in some quarters by his Pseudonym "Masaihead". He is the author of a poetry collection; *Behold, Your Scented Daughters* (2011), and a Civil Servant living in Abuja, Nigeria. Ex- Chairman, Ex- officio and Ex-Public Relations Officer of the Association of Nigerian Authors (ANA), and former National Vice Chairman of the Northern Nigerian Writers Summit (NNWS). He writes poetry, short stories, novels, drama and essays, and an award winner of the maiden Pen Nigeria/Saraba Poetry Prize, and honorable mention in the Korean Nigeria Poetry Prize 2011 & 12 respectively. Highly anthologized and influenced by the works of Toni Kan, HelonHabila, Garcia Marquez, Ben Okri, Isabel Allende, Margaret Artwood, Pablo Neruda, MaikNwosu and ToyinAdewale Gabriel. He is a Fellow of the Ebedi International Writers Residency. His writing idea is taken from a solemn believe in the triumph of the Human spirit; informed from the fact that no matter how long the night may be, morning always comes. His short story "The Front of the Past" has been accepted in the From Africa With Love Anthology. He resides at his home "Purple Rain Suite" in Abuja with his wife Rahmah five children and dog Tokyo. He can be reached at omaleabduljabbar@gmail.com, twitter: @allenabduljabbar, instagram @allenomale and facebook: omale.allenabduljabbar.

THE FRONT OF THE PAST

For Wale Okediran, Helon Habila, Toni Kan, Izzia Ahmad & Dave Njoku

Aiiiicchi! A sneeze. Then he slaps himself on the back. Then he cursed. He cursed all the past leaders. Especially those who have contributed directly or indirectly to ruining the country. Then he yawned. A long powerful yawn like an exhibition of a terribly tired hippo lounging lazily at the zoo.

Also like the hippo, he never even bothered to cover his mouth. It was a very sweet yawn, one of the few things still free to man in this day and age – especially in Nigeria! The sixth oil producing country in the world where abject poverty rules the land like zombies heeding a burgle call of death.

The man. Gray haired .Tall and lanky. Terribly light in complexion as if rubbed with yellow…

Now what shall we make of him? What would you prefer?

Good! Let us make him a retired soldier, terribly bitter, battered and burdened with memories of the Nigerian civil war. And the painful hassle-bustle of everyday, of life and living.

That done, let us make of him a guard at a bank—Emeifele Redesigning Nigeria Bank PLC Kano. Then situate the Bank along Nyesom Wike Avenue in the neighbourhood of the Hotel Royal Tropicana.

He's outside. Waiting patiently where guards wait in front of banks. This day, a gray dirty day. December. The Harmattan wind reaches out a hand to scoop up fine red sand and throws it in the faces of passers-by. Now the wind has become a cyclone, whirlwind strong enough to fall down a man and even possibly carry him off for a short trip in the air, free of charge.

The world around me dey rich, people dey enjoy, he thought. *And yet I no chop inside!*

Before Before, Soja na good good work! In fact na di best work for we country…uniform nko? E correct. E clean and e bright. Kwuma dem dey pay money well well dat time. No be now we dem dey use Soja do politics. See dat Alex Bade , a whole CDS, see how e take end? How Dem go say Bandit go kidnap Soja for NDA? Abeg make ah hear word jare!

But you no be Soja now, you be mai guardi, abi you forget? A voice whispers inside of him and angrily he fires back:

Bloody Civilian! Advance to de coconut! (Advance to be recognized) *I say which war you fight? Eh answer me? Answer me right away. I say which war you fight?*

Silence.

Very angry now, he stands up suddenly. Still very smart for his age, typical of die-hard old soldiers.

In the next minute, he is going to start again, he'll start all over, to re-enact the wars – Come on! Let us give him a gun. Just toss it in the air, as if from a tree, as if from the hands of a comrade in the jungle.

…Yes Nduka throw down the SMG. Captain…move! Advance! No retreat, No Surrender. Death to the enemy forces… grrrrrr ratatata tatatata… He charges into the jungle…

Burma! Liberia! Congo! Germany! Biafra! – Look my teeth, he exposes a terribly stained tobacco and *ogogoro* -friendly dentition but no one is missing. *Look my teeth! I am a fine old man! Which of de war you fight? You wan correct my grammar".*

Silence.

Two stories up. An opened window, the assistant manager taps on the manager's shoulders, drawing his attention to the antics of the guard busy *fighting* his wars in the Kano sun.

Sergeant Amadi! Sometimes he thinks the war is still on…

But the war is still on…when you pause to think of it. The things that led to the Nigerian Civil War in the first place are still very much around us! The untold human rights issues. When you pause to look at it, it would seem that the ghost of Biafra is haunting its murderers to their early graves. Its hunting the Middle Belters, the Niger Deltans and the Yorubas. In the first instance is the massacre of the Tives in Zaki Biam and the last two cases are the loss of Ken Saro Wiwa, the renowned writer cum human right activist and Moshood Abiola ;the acclaimed winner of the freest and fairest but sadly aborted June 12 Presidential elections in Nigeria by the Babangida junta … The manager. A pro-Biafran.

Hmm! Very weighty contribution there Mr. Ekanem, but he can't keep this antics on in the Bank premises, its bad for our image and will scare away our customers.

You're right Suleiman. But he's an old man. We can't just sack him. Let's transfer him somewhere quiet.

…So if tiefs or armed robbers come now, to rub de bank, wetin you go do? You be old man – you supose to dey village de farm, wetin you think? What about de Bandit wahala wey full everywhere now? Make you go home! Old Soja fit die too.

*I be soja! No be farmer. When …*He sits down suddenly. The clowning around has tired him. Now he's thinking. An epiphany It is coming. This time to a retired and tired ex-soldier in Nigeria. An Igbo man living in the North.

When I be small piken…I no de like farm. I de like fighting for wrestling, for village…Na him my uncle visit our village for Orlu. Dat day I beat nonsense comot for Mosis head. When dem see di blood for everywhere, na him everybody con say I must to go for Lagos, to join di army – becos of stubbornness.

Silence.

Army de good dat time. Generals self no plenty like now. Na only white man fit to be General. Only Aguyi Ironsi wey get General for Congo war. No be like now.

So hope still dey for Nigeria? Wetin you tink of Tinubu wey dem just elect as President for this 2023 election?

Hope! He's still lost in the past and the questions catch him unawares.

That one no be election. Na Peter Obi nahin everybodi vote for nahim INEC con counterbalance everything givam Tinubu…

Under Babangida and Abacha, Nigeria don see pepper since independence…

O Yes! Independence. Now he's back. *First Tafawa Balewa come, Honest gentleman but de politics too much for am. Na him Soja come take over inside coup. Chukwuma Kaduna Nzeogwu! Hmmm. Dat Man! Dat man! Dat man! dem do coup for 15 January, 1966 come remove Balewa, Ahmadu Bello – kill Hausa people plenty!…*He gives up the account, Nigerian history since independence. *But honest, dem for no kill dem like dat…*

Ehen continue, abi you no remember the history again?

Leave me! Dat no be my problem now.

Wetin be your problem den?

Silence.

See de current wahala wey we dey now, no cash, no fuel, no food…dem say dem hold money for Cental bank to prevent vote buying- what of all the dollars wey politians dey share now? Why dem no go hold de dollars also? I no know why Nigerian government always jus de suffer her citizens everytime for nothing…government after government, na so so suffer we dey.

A long pause. It breaks into an in-ordinate one. The voice. The inquirer. His conscience, is finally hushed. Like a storm weathered after a long riotous night of quacking and madness.

Oga!

Yes sergeant Amadi, what is it?

Now two hours have passed since the thunder and Rain.

Oga. I thank you for de work. As you take employ me to work for de bank.

The manager is about to enter his car, driving out of the bank premises. Around, people are coming and going, some adorned in all kinds of peculiar, turbans, depicting their cadres and levels in the society and announcing without doubts of any sort that you are in the North. Kano to be precise.

So what is the problem now? I'm going out as you can see.

Oga, I wan go home.

You want casual leave?

No oga, I wan resign. To go back to my place, Orlu for East, to farm my papa land for village.

Old soldier never die! Is the war over now? You don fight finish? You were fighting again today.

Oga manager. I no fit to lie again. The discussion takes a more genial tune.

I don tire!

I no wan fight Bandit and election war add to all de war I don fight before. I dey go East!

The manager has left. He is now in the accounts session collecting his severance pay. There are tears in his eyes. Visions of the past cloud his brain with pain and sorrow.

Fighting, fighting everywhere! No be wetin our fore fathers fight Independence for be dis. Tears cascade down his eyes and his vision blurs as an old soldier battles with the front of the past. .

Omale Allen Abdul-Jabbar

BEHOLD YOUR SCENTED DAUGHTERS

For my Scented Daughters, Imani, Medina, AAliya & Malaika

Behold your scented daughters
More precious than plumb Idoma yams
And Obije meat for the day of the feast
Fathomed in water, sojourned eight moons
And two quarters in benevolent grottoes
We traded our submarine spirits
For a chance to call you Adah
Nigerian bard who dreamt us to life

Even in the deep, we heard you, welcoming us
Chanting our ancestral praise names:
Onyete, onyete ,onyeteigblaopanda
Aolokolo we ego.progeny of skywater and earth
Those who measure gold coins for their daughter brides
And freely enrich the lustre of the moon
With the palm of their hands, after sumptuous meals
Of roasted yam and palm oil

To heed your call, we went beyond the indigo
Flames of the moon, finding motion in new bodies
Floating in space, cities, places and faces
Swirl around us like petals of *frellis and canatiums*
The flowers of underwater grottoes
They urge us with their seductive scents to give up
our voyage for their eternal hymns
Of solemn sunsets, and dizzying dusk
But a rare breeze propel us along
Haloed by bits of shattered rainbow
And nostalgia

Daintily, we touched Earth for your sake!
To walk on land, to call you Adah!

This poet with eternal eyes
Sage with a thousand minds
You summoned us,
Behold your scented daughters;
Imani, Medinah, AAliay, Malaika

YOUNG SAILOR BOY

For HajiaAjumayiOjiileOmale , May 12 angels guard and guide your soul

Silence envelopes my ship of dreams
My kit of songs…
Young sailor boy sitting on the masthead
In this mist-haze and solemn cadence
Of a dreamy Harmattan night
Distant horizon, moonlight glittering on the face of the sea
I wonder, does the sea have an end?

Nomad floating from scene to séance on the runway
Of self- discovery, searching for meaning
Tonight I bear the wrapped body of my mother
To the gate of the after-life
I, whose duty it's to usher her benevolent soul
With *salaams*,
Kind words that open the gate of the after-life

Help me! Help me!! Kind merciful Gabriel
Help me! Young sailor boy; a cold chill numbs my brain
And my blood boils in my veins

Silence envelopes my ship of dreams
My kit of songs, bard devoid of words
I muster all the wind in my lungs, here at this majestic gate
Of the after-life, this terribly cold-windy night
And utter the *salaams* to open the gate of Heaven
Kind merciful Gabriel, please receive the soul of Ajumayi
Woman who believed ultimately in God.

BEHOLD YOUR RAINBOW SON

For Omale Rayyan Abduljabbar

Welcome the one who comes
With a fist clenched with Rainbow
Face bearing the tangerine-amber glow
Of sunset
Stars in my teeth!
You're dashing Rainbow son

Alone with my mother
On cold Ramadan nights
Hands raised in prayers
Hearts beating to the Om twang
Of the Orient
Fervently, you entreated for me
Behold your Rainbow child
Son, friend, brother
Completer of circles

Fashioned from cool calming sweet breeze
And the rarest of nectarine
Fashioned from rhythms of pebbled lake
And the softest of purple
I am the memo of the genie in the bottle
The smile bringer
Behold
Your Rainbow son!

THE YOUNGER SISTER I NEVER HAD

Like Obu, who laments of his brother
More precious than moonlight
Aatuma, I want you to know
That I follow the cranes at twilight
Of dusk, searching for you
To the end spheres of the nimbus clouds
In the East.

I named you after the one whose hopes never waned
Our grandma, Aatuma
My heart craves eternally for you

When I dream, I plait your dark-rich hair
Side by side, we ride on gentle Pegasus
To run errands for Ajumayi
Our mother
When I wake, I encounter you in echoing whispers
Of whispering grooves

When I travel, I look for you
In the exultant hymns
Of wayside flora and fauna
And the emergent epiphanies
of the endless road that goes
Beyond man`s farthest
Destinations

When I fall in love, I look for you
In the guile-less laughter of indigo flames
Floating Genie at three scores and six seasons
Wherever the Heigdeggerian lure of the open spaces

Have driven me
I look for you Aatuma
The younger sister I never had

I CARRY SOME DREAMS IN THE TRUNK OF MY CAR

I carry some dreams in the trunk of my car
Like petrol trapped in a Jerry can
I fear that they`ll explode

Like rats in a ceiling, I hear them rattling
When I'm stuck in traffic
Their photo-kinesis and effervescence
Overheat my car and burn-out my top gasket

A multiplicity of data, feelings, desires
Schemes, memories, fears, secrets…
Poetry and photographs framed in portraits;
Morning rush, urban torrential,
Rustic blisses, sleepyheads…
Stories frozen like a Kodak moment-
My heart beats in tune

I carry some dreams in the trunk of my car
Day in day out commuting to work
Everyday stuck in traffic jams
Stroking my rites of passage

TRINIDAD AND TOBAGO

My Baby woman!
Why don't you be Trinidad?
And I,
Tobago!
Two Islands forever
Joined,
As one.
There's music playing
On harps, drifting slowly
From invisible Genies
A lucid wind defies time
Blowing softly
From the lips of Trinidad
To Tobago.
The land is purpled from
Happy tears of Angels
And the samba, salsa and calypso
That you hear is your heart
And mine tangoed forever in a duet
The world will end
Tomorrow,
But no! My baby!
Not for us.
If only you'll be Trinidad
And I,
Tobago!

TUAREG

For Abdul Omale

My life is a house
Hollowed by the wind
Like a tent in the wilderness
My silk soul dangles in the breeze
Between the dialogue of sky and dust

Nomad at three scores
And six seasons, forever afflicted
With the lure of the open spaces

I am the bottled genie and the memo
Quietly awaiting discovery,
Watching life's mysteries denuded
Slowly like hourglass sand.

Memories of my childhood ambush me like
A web of sins:
All the friends I used to know
But can no longer see…
What was new once and alluring
But soon grew old and tattered and alas, gone!
Bodies I've swam in, caves I've hidden in...

And Poetry o Poetry! Tiny persistent spirit,
Your medium in which we say it best,
Damn you!

I am the purple breath of a Tuareg's dream
Floating between the dialogue of sky and dust

Quietly awaiting discovery;
Searching for meaning.

NOMAD @45

March 31st, Abuja 2016,Happy birthday to me

At four scores and five seasons
I stand and stare at the fire of lifetimes
Flaming before my eyes
In the Terra Cotta mission
Of Bedouin skies
One left behind by the caravan
My tongue speaks only of eternal
Prayers for rain

Like an Oasis in the cool of the night
In perpetual communion with starlight
Visions of Mama`s grave   remain
'Abdul, why do you cry?
Has God not done enough for you?'
Her words echo to me

Today at four scores and five seasons
I spread my mat in the sand
Face facing Mecca, in the most solemn cadence
I pray for mum and dad
I pray for the blessing of my loins
I pray for my siblings
I pray for my life`s journey
Through this ache and emptiness
For my eyes to stop stinging
My heart to finally regain it's rythm
And be at peace with itself again

UNDER THE NYANYA BRIDGE

7thMay Abuja 2021

Like copulating smoke
In traffic under the Nyanya bridge
I watch my dreams waft out of the trunk
of my car, for a while,
Mingling with the dreams of others;
The Hajia in the beaten Lexus jeep
Hands tap tapping on the wheel
Hijab of orange blossoms -
Abdulrahman in Massachusetts,
Where will I get the money for his rent?
Zarah in Cyprus ....how to complete
Her tuition
If only they can get the scholarship,…
Starting a Barbing saloon business, where do I get
an honest barber?
"Oya move I say, keep this lane speeding"
The Soldier with the big gun utters
And I watch the various dreams
Of commuters retreat again into various trunks
of cars, each to their owners
Delicately, we glide on,
Peddling ourplethora of worries.

THE NIGHT IS FILLED WITH FLOWERS

At the kitchen, dicing peppers
Onions and tomatoes
Making dinner,
I am thinking of you.

Outside, the Jos breeze is gentle
The night is filled with flowers
But the scent of you is what I perceive the most
Smelling my hand for whiffs of you
When we shook outside your gate
Saying goodnight.

Now, the oil is frying in the pan
I am thinking of you, walking you home
In the rain;
Blue jeans
White shirt
And low cut hair

Half minded, I pour the vegetables
Thinking of you…

I hear the sound of eagles cachinnating
On stretched ease wings, I hear the sound
Of waterfalls dropping on shores
Covered with blue seas shells

Thinking of you, making dinner
Tonight, there`re liquid ribbons in my eyes
I am remembering the thrill of eyes closed
On the lazy boy, I am travelling down

A dazzling beam of light
I am remembering;
love

Section Two

Seun Osho

Seun Osho is a writer and creative entrepreneur from Abuja, Nigeria. He is a writer, majorly of poetry and short stories, a stylist, freelance editor and the creative director of both his fashion brand and another online lifestyle project called Underbridge. Seun has recently moved to Lagos seeking new challenges and a change of scenery from his home city, Abuja.

THEY DON'T MAKE GREAT MOVIES ANYMORE

I hadn't had a cigarette in six days and I'm not exactly suffering withdrawals. I prayed today, I don't know why. This is my second day of trying to write this week and I can't stop thinking about finding a way to sneak magnolia into this episode; it's such a cool, romantic word. It sounds like a strain of a recreational drug, or a type of tree, maybe it should be the name of a fragrance; it could be the name of a place. Magnolia could be the name of a princess or a blunt wrap flavour. To me, Magnolia is a pink hue of the pastels familiar to yeezy colour ways; it's the colour of boy meets girl emotions, like the flavoured creamy center of your favourite confectionery.

I've been pretty reclusive lately, nothing mysterious but just a whole lot of nose picking, not showering and living like a hermit. It's like I'm depressed, but without the self loathing, so I know it's not depression- or is it?

Anyway, as I was saying, I smoked a cigarette today. I met a girl at a bar and took one when she offered as I joined her table at this music release and listening party in Jabi. I couldn't let her smoke alone; it felt rude to turn her down. No woman had offered me a smoke before. She was great, thank God. She's the kind of girl songs are written about, not because she's anything out of the ordinary to look at, but her aura was strong; a difficult woman to forget. This brings me to my latest dilemma titled after my favourite movie at the moment "the object of my affection". Jennifer Aniston is like a dream in that movie. It's an interesting and almost too real story about how feelings actually work if you didn't know. It's a realistic tale of what I assume is a hypothetical situation, but for once, I could appreciate the humanized portrayal of a homosexual man in a movie, without having to watch desperation bubble to the surface. It didn't look like exploitation of an agenda to sell a story. It was just a great story about love and life. Its brilliant; a must-watch!

I want one of those, you know?! An object of my affection, someone new to love -cue Hozier's someone new- but I can't seem to stop wondering about my exes;

I think about Afro and if she's forgiven me. I wonder, would we'll keep it real and go chicken republic if we ran into each other on the street of Lagos. I hope we don't have unresolved feelings, especially if our chance meeting is in Ikoyi or VI. Unresolved feelings can be quite expensive.

I also wonder about Fay. I think it was the sex. I didn't devour her beautiful body when she let me have her and then I didn't try to make up for it or fight for her when her unspoken disappointment drove us apart. When she tried to break up with me, I only got mad because I knew how she talked about her exes with me and the idea of her talking about me like that to someone else drove me crazy. In retrospect, I should have fought instead. That's what a real man does, I think; he seeks security at all cost for the woman he loves; but I didn't fight. I was afraid to be vulnerable, I was certain she would fuck me with a hot curling iron. I cut her off instead, completely. I miss her sometimes.

Bacon, the actual love of my life. My favorite infatuation. I don't want to talk about bacon. I have refused to do anything about how I feel about her beyond telling her – This pattern of cowardice has me rolling my eyes too – Who knew it'll be so hard finding somebody to love and it only gets harder. You have to get them to let you love them, after that, you can only hope that the object of your affection reciprocates while you jump through hoops to become the person they deserve- I'm hard on myself, I know, but don't worry, I'm too lazy to drive myself over the edge.

I almost forgot about Americanah. I should have let her give me that rim job in retrospect. Americanah was the one I'd hoped I'd save and ride off into the sunset with. The sex was amazing, most times it felt like standing under a waterfall, other times I could have sworn there was yoghurt on my pubes. She tasted like roasted almonds sweetened by marshmallows and smelled how I imagine magnolia must, but, alas, I wasn't ready to ride or die for a woman who didn't trust me enough to tell me when she cheated. I didn't have the patience to earn her trust in the midst of her betrayal and somehow, once again, it seems being a man took just that. Patience. How was I supposed to feel, knowing she literally seduced the man who introduced us while we were keeping our relationship a secret? If I were one to fantasize about marriage he'd have been on the train.

Babe, you should have told me.

Bacon made me take down her photo last week over some tweets and it hurt, but she's still talking to me, so I don't know how to feel. She has so much power over me and I feel like nothing will ever be good enough for Bacon, including myself or anyone else. Sometimes I think my infatuation with her might be unhealthy and that by now, if you're still reading this, you too like amebo -laughs awkwardly- I really don't want to talk about Bacon, in fact we don't talk anymore. I lied.

REBLS REBELS: ESSENTIALLY, QUE SERA SERA]

I don't skate,
It stirs a conundrum of excitement and fear
I shouldn't break bones for sport
My mama fi go break some more

Used to play street ball,
wrestled a man or two;
but I no too sabi,
Last last, no be every black man fi be Ali

Pencils, pens & brushes,
that's my forte
A man has been a sloth,
quite unfortunate

Cheers to Hunger
and thirst
Discomfort gives
innovation birth

Jaara e
Butty ni mi,
ma lo gawk e
Etiquette mi wa premium,

5 stars!

Mafo!

Still, I'm formidable in the bush
and well known in the streets

I pray for the artisans;
"Graffiti on the wall, on the skin
It's all the same
God is Mario Puzzo,
Chinua Achebe is the Messiah.
We do not abide by mortal rules
If you're reading this,
the world is yours. Amen!"

She said I don't belong here,
I asked her "who does?"
We're all surviving the best we can

925ers are hyenas
Be careful, concrete jungle
of aired invoices,
they water down peace.

I caught them,
Phony ponies are obvious
They strut dramatically

Endangered species *l'ómò*
Real

Olopa,
steady poaching

O su mi but ko rera

It's fuck everyone out here,
Rude boy, look sharp;

Na only your mama love you.

THE WHITE HOUSE

It was a wet Thursday night when I walked into the White House at the foot of the hill. Inside, I was greeted by familiar phenomena. I am certain I had never experienced these beings before, yet they were familiar and comfortable. They took the forms of the ghosts of my ancestor, my offspring and my nemesis, all eating together. "Join us, there is enough food!" they said, beckoning in unison. I obliged them; hunger regards no one and has no shame after all.

We wined and dined heartily for a precious endless moment while time seemed to stand still; we took turns sharing tales. They told me stories about my future and shed light on my present predicaments, and then I told them about my past. Each of us was amazed by the stories the others told. I knew now why they felt so familiar. They were me and I was them, we were all present yet we existed in alternate times and dimensions. The house rumbled. A mild collision of universes could cause that. Might we leave a cosmic microwave background behind, I wondered. The only thing I knew for sure was that I knew nothing. I'd become a sponge. Everything here was new to me.

The one that was my offspring shared my fiery resilience and had the heart of a Gemini woman, just like my mother. He spoke in a comforting opera, an onomatopoeia of sorts; it was through his pen it seemed, I could hear his song. It was there he bared his vulnerabilities; completely oblivious of his fragile countenance and without his mask of boastful speaking. In fact, when all was penned and done, I knew who he was through and through. At first, through his verbiage my faith in the benevolence of mankind was restored. Not long after, said faith was dashed. Again. "Very well," I'd said to myself "he is just a young man."

My nemesis had eyes the color of mischief and lips coated with a film of caution. He said his chest was made of bulletproof glass and I could see his heart was wrapped in a Jolly Roger carrying two skulls; a woman and a child. He dared me to enter the grand line, subtly announcing he was after the one piece, man's eternal purpose. This man, uninterested in shedding his child-like demeanor even though he communicated in sagely simple sentences, challenged my very existence. He was many things I wanted to be as a child. A man must fight many battles in the name of legacy; I am grateful for this one. Bless the multiverse for serving up a worthy opponent in the same being as a friend.

My ancestor stood tall and large; his kind demeanor took nothing away from his strong, manly presence. He relayed tales of growth and hope. My chest swelled with pride at the stories he told. A man who was me before I became me, who has stood where I stand and walked ahead of the path I'm on, eating, drinking and laughing in conversation, fulfilled by his resilience. Now he had fathered some and become lord over others, remaining unperturbed by the waves of the world that crashed and thrashed away at men like us. My faith in myself was restored. Thank you.

I walked into a White House with a black gate at the foot of a hill last week and I was all alone, but the least lonely I'd felt in a long time. Cheerful hallucinations manifested introspective simulations; over and over I sought answers my eyes couldn't find. This may be the onset of psychosis; I have always had doubts concerning my sanity, but maybe, just maybe it was nothing to worry about. Maybe it was just a vision from God and his friends.

Section Three

Ayo Oyeku

Ayo Oyeku is a fellow of Ebedi International Writers Residency. He made an early mark in 2004, when his first chapter book was selected by World Bank for distribution across schools and libraries in Nigeria. Subsequently, his poems began to appear in several anthologies and journals, including Brittle Paper, AFREADA, VINYL, Kalahari Review, The Sky is Our Earth, According to Sources (Writers Project of Ghana, 2015), Experimental Writing: Volume 1, Africa vs Latin America Anthology. In 2015, his young-adult novel, Tears of the Lonely, won the Ezenwa Ohaeto Prize for Fiction, by the Society of Young Nigerian Writers. In 2016 and 2018, he was a finalist of the prestigious Golden Baobab Prize, in the Early Chapters category. In 2019, he won the Association of Nigerian Authors prize for children's literature, for his book, Mafoya and the Finish line. In 2021, he published his eight children's book, Queen Moremi Makes a Promise. Ayo Oyeku is contributor for World Kid Lit, member of the Society for Children's Book Writers and Illustrators, and the founder of the creative publishing firm, Eleventh House.

THE MAGIC JALABIYA

Gusts of wind swept through the streets that Monday morning. Grains of sand scurried across the ground, and small pebbles rattled against a flattened carton. A small hand emerged from beneath the carton, flipping it over to reveal a boy. He smoothened his faded, oversized shirt with his palms and bent over to put on his ratty black trainers.

Hamza looked across the empty street and back at the abandoned filling station which had become his home. His gaze rested on a worn sheet of cardboard. He moved towards it and kicked it sideways. A second boy scrambled to his feet. He was shorter and darker than Hamza. An old dirty V-neck T-shirt covered his dry, scabby skin. "Morning Komandant!" Bashir raised his arm and saluted.

"You slept for too long," Hamza said.

Bashir looked down at his bare feet.

There was a short silence. Their hungry eyes roamed the stains and holes on each other's shirts then their cheeks swelled. Deep laughter from their empty bellies cracked the silence. They hugged each other and the joy of being alive swept over them.

The early morning clouds slid under the sun. The boys hurried to the back of the filling station to pick up their food bowls which were attached to long strings, so the children could carry them across their bodies. They hung tote bags over their foreheads like they had seen school children do.

As they wandered through their neighbourhood, they saw an old beggar curled up on the sidewalk. They had never seen him before. The boys wrinkled their noses. The beggar's rags stank. He looked like he was about to die of hunger.

"Let's hurry." Hamza said, tugging Bashir's sleeve.

Three turns to the left and two to the right led them into Sokoto Central Area. Street traders were setting up their stalls. Cars honked. Traffic lights blinked. People heading to work brushed past them.

"We are here," Hamza said, raising his chin. He liked to state the obvious.

The two boys joined a queue of homeless children at the entrance of a big, black gate. The children screamed when the gate screeched open. An elderly woman came out with a sack full of plastic food packs. One after the other, she handed them to the children with a small smile on her face. Hamza collected his pack with a quiet thank you while Bashir hurried to open his. It was their favourite — tuwo shinkafa with a piece of meat as big as their ears.

They raced through the popular market to the filling station. At first, Bashir touched every stall they rushed past with the tips of his fingers. When they got to the fruit section of the market, he swiped some bananas and oranges from a table and stuffed them into his tote bag. The fruit-seller yelled, 'thieves!' He cursed and he ran after them.

Hamza and Bashir picked up speed. They knew every corner of the market. They curved round stalls, slid under tables, jumped over benches and squeezed through gates. A few more market-sellers joined in the chase. "Barawo banza!' they shouted.

Just before they got to the path that led to the main road, Bashir lost his footing and tripped over. His food pack spilled out of his bag, and the contents disappeared under a cloud of dust. Hamza's nose was covered in beads of sweat. It was as if the air around him had suddenly got warmer. He halted and rushed to Bashir's side.

"We are almost there," Hamza said, pulling Bashir to his feet.

Hamza swung Bashir's right arm around his shoulder and dragged him along. With the angry traders closing in on them, they arrived at the hidden entrance of a familiar tunnel.

The tunnel smelt like sewage, but the boys had perfected the act of holding their breath. As they moved through the dark tunnel, they teased each other about the funny things they had done during the chase. Peels of their laughter filtered through the dampness.

When the coast was clear, they crawled out onto the streets and filled their lungs with fresh, clean air. They linked arms and headed back to the filling station.

"He is still here," Bashir whispered, his eyes on the old beggar.

"Let's talk to him," said Hamza.

Bashir was hesitant but he let Hamza to drag him towards the old man.

They stood next to the old beggar and waved the swooping flies away. His heavy breathing made his chest rise and collapse beneath the rags. Hamza nudged him gently on the shoulder but the old man did not respond. Bashir prodded him on the leg. Still nothing. Hamza stared down at the beggar's long toenails.

Bashir's brow folded into a frown when Hamza reached into his tote bag for his food pack. He knew what Hamza was about to do. He remembered that he had already lost his food pack. As they walked away, he tried to hide his disappointment. Not even a small chunk of meat would pass his lips that day.

"When he wakes up, at least he'll have something to eat," Hamza said.

In their make-shift abode, they sat in a corner quietly and shared the stolen fruits. Hamza peeled off the skin of a banana. He suggested that they go to a different part of town on their next outing. Bashir nodded. They knew that some of the traders would be looking for them.

The oranges were juicy and the guavas were firm. With food in their bellies, the boys soon fell asleep.

***

Hamza's eyes flew open. There was a presence like a shadow hovering around and over them. He rubbed his eyes. Standing before him was the old beggar. Hamza nudged Bashir to wake him but Bashir just turned over and inserted his thumb into his open mouth.

The beggar had a smile on his face. A robe draped from his outstretched arms. Hamza pinched Bashir until he stirred, yawned and opened his eyes.

"Being kind has its rewards." The beggar's cheeks collapsed into his angular face, as he spoke.

Hamza's lips trembled.

"This is my gift to you." The old beggar's eyes sparkled.

Hamza jumped to his feet to collect a green jalabiya with gold embroidery running from its collar to its chest. Fancy stitching adorned the cuffs and the hem of the robe. The boys stared at it. It was not like any jalabiya they had seen before.

"This is a magic jalabiya, Hamza. When you put it on, call it twice and command it to take you anywhere you want to go. It will grant your wish," the beggar said.

Hamza wondered how the old beggar knew his name.

"All you have to do is hold each other's hands and the magic jalabiya will take both of you wherever you wish," the beggar added. He looked from Hamza to Bashir, and back.

The boys watched as the old beggar turned to walk away. He walked past the old concrete slabs. He made a small curve around the almond tree behind the filling station. He ambled down a dirt road until he faded from sight.

"Do you think he was telling the truth?" Hamza asked, eyeing the robe suspiciously.

"We won't know unless we try it." Bashir said, straightening up.

Hamza took off his shirt. He shut his eyes as he slipped the magic jalabiya over his head. Suddenly, tiny bubbles rose out of the robe and filled the air around him. His matted hair stood up, his eyes became as bright as the moon, and his skin looked like it was sprinkled with glitters.

Perhaps the old beggar was not lying, he thought.

Bashir could tell his friend had been empowered with something strange but amazing. He became excited.

"We should test the jalabiya," Bashir suggested, picking up his food bowl and tote bag.

"Where should we go?" Hamza asked. He was nervous and excited at the same time.

They had lived in Sokoto all their lives. They had heard fantastic tales about Lagos from the lips of strangers. They had also seen pictures of Aso Rock, and knew it is where the President lived.

"We have never been anywhere except here." Bashir said, as he ran his fingers over his friend's new robe.

Hamza picked up his food bowl and tote bag, but paused when he saw a sturdy man approaching in the distance. They were not sure if they had met him before. But as soon as the man spotted them, he shouted, "Aren't you the boys who stole from the market this morning?"

The boys looked at each other without a word. Their cover had been blown. As the man started running towards them, they grabbed each other's hands. Hurriedly, Hamza gave the command,

Magic jalabiya!
Magic jalabiya!
Take us to the bank of the nearest river!

The boys were spun into a ring of sparkling bubbles. They screamed as an unseen force sucked them through a doorway with green, white and gold lights. That was the last thing they remembered, as they vanished.

The sturdy man screamed with shock. He turned around and fled.

*This is an extract from the forthcoming chapter book, **The Magic Jalabiya.***

OMALE AND THE MAGIC PAINTBRUSH

Long time ago, there was a hardworking painter in a small town named Omale. He was kind and helpful to everyone around him. Although Omale worked very hard, every day, yet he wasn't wealthy.

One morning, Omale believed he struck gold when the famous and wealthy trader, Abdul-Jabbar, asked him to paint his mother. Gladly and patiently, Omale started the work before sunrise and completed it before sunset. Eagerly, he went to Abdul-Jabbar's house to deliver the painting. The look on the wealth trader's face showed that he was pleased with the painting but in return he offered Omale a paltry amount as his wages.

Omale was displeased but he collected the money. That was all his family would feed on for a few days. As he strolled back home, he found a shiny object on the floor. He stopped and picked it up.

"Ah, it's a paintbrush." Omale said, putting the paintbrush in his pocket.

That night, Omale used the paintbrush to draw a red apple. When he finished, a juicy red apple appeared in front of him. He was surprised and eager to see what else the brush could do. So he began to paint several other things. He painted a table and some chairs and they all appeared in his house. Hs wife and children were pleased by the gift the gods had brought their way. Omale painted big apples, took them to the market and sold them. He spent the money on inks of all colors so he could paint several things he desired.

Soon enough, Omale had all he desired. He painted himself a new and better house, clothes, shoes and everything he could think of. Rather than keep the magic brush to himself, he started using it to help his neighbors and friends. Every morning, Omale would paint a feast of food for his neighbors.

One morning while he was drawing, Abdul-Jabbar sent some thugs to attack Omale and steal the magic paintbrush. And they succeeded. Late at night, Abdul-Jabbar spread a big canvas out and painted a huge pile of money.

"I will paint this canvas till my paint finishes so that my money will be plenty. I will be the wealthiest man in this village and everywhere," he said to himself as he painted.

When he ran out of paint, he stepped back and waited for the money to appear. Sadly, the pile of money did not appear. Abdul-Jabbar sent his thugs to bring Omale before him, and they did. When they arrived, Abdul-Jabbar gave the paintbrush to Omale and told him to paint him a big mansion, horses, fertile farmlands and a lot of money. Omale painted the greedy man everything he wanted and a pile of money on an island surrounded by water.

Abdul-Jabbar was angry that he could not reach the money so he ordered Omale to paint him a boat. And he did. The greedy man got on the boat saying;

"When I come back, you will paint me all the money and the gold in the world."

When the boat reached a far distance, Omale painted tides in the river. The tides swept the boat far away to an unknown destination, where Abdul-Jabbar suffered for everything and had no way of coming back.

Omale returned home and invited everybody to his mansion. They all ate, sang and danced. From that day, they all lived in peace and prosperity.

THE RACE

Once upon a time, there were two friends – the hare and the rabbit. They loved each other, went to school together, studied together, and also played together at the park. Wherever you find the hare, the rabbit will be too. And when it was time to sleep, both always found it hard to bid each other goodnight.

One day while they were playing in the park, the rabbit realized he could burrow and hide inside holes faster than the hare. This gave him a surge of confidence and he challenged his friend to a race.

"A race? Why?" The hare asked.

"To know the best runner between us."

"I don't think this is a good idea."

The hare discouraged but the rabbit won't let go. He insisted on having a race with the hare, else he will not be friends with him again.

That evening, when the hare returned home, he was worried. He could not eat his snack of carrot and cabbage. He was smothered in thoughts, "if I don't race with rabbit, he won't be my friend again. If I race him and win, he won't be happy and he might stop being my friend. I don't want to lose our friendship, so I will race him and let him win just like I do all the time in the park."

On their way to school the following morning, the hare agreed to race with the rabbit, but warned that it must be between them, nobody should be informed. The rabbit said nothing. To the hare's surprise, as they entered into the school compound, he realized that almost everyone in school was aware of the race contest. Stuck across walls, doors and notice boards were posters captioned,

Rabbit versus Hare:
Who is the best runner?
Find out on Saturday!

The hare felt very bad and was sad all day. He tried to talk to rabbit but he was busy inviting spectators to the race at the park. All through the week the rabbit did not speak to the hare in the school. And every time he checked the rabbit at home, he met his absence. A day to the contest, the hare wrote a small note and left it at rabbit's door. Written on the note was:

Rabbit, I know I can run better than you.

I've always allow you to win whenever we race in the park.

And tomorrow, I will allow you to win again because of our friendship.

When the rabbit saw the note, he smiled, scoffed and trashed it.

The hare was met with a wave of shock when he got to the park. The loud spectators were chanting, "Rabbit! Rabbit!! Rabbit!!!" The rabbit with a swelled head. And he pranced and jumped around with a fervor of excitement and boundless energy. As no one noticed his arrival, the hare sat quietly under the tree watching his friend.

"I won't let that smile go away, I will make sure he wins," The hare whispered to himself.

When the race was about to begin, the hare tried to say hello to the rabbit but he turned away from him with a grump.

"On your marks!

Get set!

Go!!!"

The race began. The rabbit took off with all his might while the crowd screamed his name, the hare decided to run as slow as he could. The rabbit, enjoying the lead, decided to look back and mock his friend, unfortunately he tripped over a pebble and fell. Seeing this, the hare rushed to help him. The rabbit was quite hurt, and the race was brought to an end.

The following morning, the hare sat beside his friend as the doctor examined his ankle and elbow.

"You have nothing to worry about. It's just a little sprain. You will be up in no time." The doctor assured.

"Thanks Doc." They chorused.

Later that week, when rabbit's foot healed, he went to the hare's house and said,

"Dear friend, I am very sorry, I have been a bad friend."

The hare was happy he had realized his mistakes and apologized.

"Our friendship is more important than the race." The hare stated.

"Yes it is," the rabbit replied.

The two hugged each other. From that day on, their friendship grew stronger than it was before the race.

Section Four

Nosakhare Collins

Nosakhare Collins (he/him) is a Nigerian poet, writer, publisher, editor, literary critic, documentary photographer, researcher, and tutor. He is the CEO/Managing Director/Founding Editor of Libretto Publishers Limited, the parent company of Libretto Magazine, a journal of arts, Libretto Bookstores, an independent publishing company. He is a fellow of the Ebedi International Writers Residency. He is the author of *"a pilgrim of songs"*, *"a song of endless flames"*, *"when ravens become flowers"* and *"a symphony of existential profundity"*. Works have appeared in National dailies and International online as well as in print journals, newspapers and anthologies such as *Salmon Creek Journal, Wingless Dreamer Publisher, Odd Magazine, Journal of erato, Openwork Magazine, Libero America Poetry, Rejection Letter Journal, Ebedi Review, The Newcastle Review, New Telegraph, Least Bittern Books, Poetry Festival, Indian Periodical Journal, Writers Space Africa, Antarctica Journal, Litpoint Africa Magazine, Sevhage Review, Youth Shade Magazine, Alabama's Best Emerging Poet Anthology 2019, Best "New" African Poets Anthology 2018, 2019 & 2020, Association of Nigerian Authors (ANA), Africa vs Latin America Anthology 2020, A Collection of poems; For Ikeogu, For Poetry: Anthology of Poems in Honour of Ikeogu Oke, 84 Delicious Bottle of Wine for Wole Soyinka Anthology, InnerChild Press Anthology 2020,*

OPA Anthology 2020(USA), *Songs For The Weaverbird: An Anthology of Writing and Art in Celebration of Christopher Okigbo, and several others.* He was awarded in the 3rd Chinua Achebe Poetry/Essay Prize by The Society of Young Nigerian Writers, and also, he was longlisted for the 2020 Prof. Idris Amali Ekphrastic Poetry Prize by Nasara Creative. His works have been translated to French, Italian, Spanish and others. Read more about Nosakhare via www.nosakharecollins.com

EBEDI WHISPERING TREE

i want to write you into a book—
a poem
as i sit underneath this tree
my legs crossed each other
feeling the breeze
wave zigzaggedly
and my feet unstable—
s h a k i n g
i don't intend to be a supper
to this tremendous afternoon cold
for my body is not
a refinement of waste metaphor

i want to dance to your gong
—a sonorous sound
play me those songs the hunters sang
in the forest of Iseyin
let me hear the rhythm
and let it flow like the river of Babylon
as praise elude the cloud with a fad sound
for it is a taboo not to visit your land
and hear not a single song of you
 singing in my tongue
for are you not the goddess of songs
—the hunter sang in the forest
that was named after the hunter
for are you not the orchestrator—
the songs that have led me into this tree

i wanted to write you in my song—
for the people of Iseyin

and in the Aseyin palace
where queens and kings will sing with me

as i seat underneath this tree
taking little sip of guava
and writing you a poem
that reads like a forest song
for i will someday read it when i visit again
but before that day comes
i want to feel and embrace your beauty
as i plug my earpiece into the ear
listening to fela kuti song *"water no get enemy"*.
while the birds' chip and hum on the tree

SPOKEN RIVER

the faces bear the last names
of a broken heart stroke with grief
as we hear the spirit of streams cry
louder with signs of puddles into the heart

tears are weighted with felicity, floating
always on earth, soaked with sudden joy
for happiness obeys the law of heaviness
and gutted like sadness, and become normal

every sound has a height, to face the pap
with sound tiptoeing into a sea, rocking the
broken ribs, and smiling back at flowing waters
seeking land to calm our furious soul

there are no too much words that hold sorrows
the vast needs to be broken, stable to tear off
the sound breaking into puddles
as every river breaks into the spirit of spoken waters

here, we hear the river speaks of felicity
when it begins to flow more, breaking into
qualified part, and seeking into the land
as earth is waiting to hear the river speak its language

dumdumdum..
let the world hear of you
& let your greatness manifest
dumdumdum..
& let our heart be the history to be told
perhaps a new dawn
will speak of it

ONE BODY

look at the stars. even at night
they are beautiful

wrought from tiny love. the brightness
is inside you, open
at the bottom of today.

you will see, you only need
love to understand the future.

the work of crushing tomatoes
were always prayers,
one body to everything, broken to liquid.

MY BODY

my body is a traveler
that seeks love and affection
journeying away from afar
carries us,
the sun & moon
and every city shine in light & dark

i need hope to stay long in this body
where love is denied
and covered in molested farewell

i need hope to stay & survive
the bones left in my body are already wrinkly shacking
and i am still hoping to live longer

above my roof i hear silence drumming sadness
in my head
        and a soft sound of death descending –
and when i tried falling asleep again,
or probably try running towards the door
a shadow of myself ran towards me
shouting for help
and i was right there thinking it was a reflection
from another being
but it was i,
who was standing close to my body
shouting for help

REFLECTIONS

you've melted my heart with pain and anytime i look deep
into your eyes
i keep bleeding
and it won't stop gushing out

i can't get why my body reflects on your sadness
i see it clearly now
and i believe you too can see it

there's something sinister here that i can't lay a finger on
something malevolent
it dies and resurrects from its slump

the world is a reflection of you
it's always been yet you insist i breathe under your
sophisticated care
and therefore, i need air too

it seems you need to forget your past and stop hurting us
with it while we sleep
we are not aliens who forget pains easily
we are more like a shadow of ourselves hidden from the
valley of truth

these eyes blink pain each time you arrive
the pain is too irksome
you look devilish when you smile gorgeously

everyone saw your smile
devilish and malevolent heart
oh, it seems i too wasn't late,

the world saw it too

the mirror knows how to show us the truth
every time we stand and stare at our conscious body
it knows we are reflections of our problems

SEASONS

silence is one part of speech that carries war
as it carries sorrow and chaos.
a man's voice echoes through lonely
ear, a boy's voice rising so close
to the road, shouting for help, a girl's voice
screaming furiously inside the room
her uncle forced her body to the wall
beside the bed; the voice seems
to be shouting not mourning, like its drums define resistance.
surviving speaks with one voice which is hope, water speaks
in clear form which is wet and fluid.
some seasons gather chaos that leads to war
our lives are mapped around this cycle.
i am yet to understand
why some seasons gather sand of war

REMEMBER THEIR NAMES

don't forget to hold them where life pierces them
for they would not forget you either
for their life asterisks in your life
for they are boys of the hood
but when a boy dies today, you will regret
the offer you forget to give him
when he came crawling at your doorstep,
he came with both legs broken
by a soldier who cocked his gun into his body
sleeping in his parents' arms
waking up to see faces of different doctors
piercing his body with needles
sometimes, life is unable to give answers to questions
because the earth is spurious
of living beings with furious hearts
perhaps, this is it, what we don't know
of what darkness chants us
but remember that boy who crawled to you
begging for home and benevolence
to fetch a little from the softness of your heart
but remember that boy's name that needed godly help
for his freedom is laying within your balm

APRIL

i remember when our voices pitched
and our faces collapsed into different thoughts
and angered – the mirror of your silence
your grief asleep in bed every night
i remember how the morning brought casket of loved ones
who went to war
and then our desires to be happy chanted with sorrow
and our body went ferry; south, east, west and north
distance tries to kiss our feet with forgetfulness
try to plunge the bruised away
and erase the heat and pain of history
i have come to colour hope
with the ice of your survival
i have held your burning tears in the rain

SINGING SONGS IN WINDOW TO THE MOON

she stares at the oriel
where her daughter spent the night
the other day she'd forgotten her
lost in the memory of the pitch
because her plastic life caved in her years in school
and window is where a truth is
known, and the moon could be, where all
colors can be seen
and truth could be reveal

she walks out to join the daughter
following all the steps where truth
can be seen easily. the day carries
grief and holds on a cold day is like
nothing can see — a vague smile
the joy turns grief, dark open
a shape already given a sign
a small sigh,
that dark songs are never might to be sung

XERODERMA PIGMENTOSUM

/pɪg mən'toʊ səm/ [pig-muh n-toh-suh m]

1. When i told my parents my strength is failing me,
the sun has rejected my feelings & good friends'
thoughts have kept me indoor silent
& depressed
they look at me like a little boy who is yet to believe Christ
exist
like Christ was up in heaven staring at me
about to wish and rain me a litany of heal songs
their smile opens a hallow in their cheeks
as if god will come down & heal me quickly
from what is already meant to die in this body
i couldn't imagine but how confused it was for me
when mother stared at me and said a few words of
encouragement;

a hypotenuse of darkness that is inside you
we can't lose you now
& hope you fight to survive.

she calls it a hypotenuse of darkness
and sees it as enemy
& calls on god every opportunity
but she forgets it's as a result of a defect

when a body shows unhealthy symptoms
healing cannot be set on the body
if the body is on fire
it's like the earth's debris

& perhaps already said,
you cannot heal what's already quenching

& this is a disorder
no medical practitioner
can heal
not even your gods
you can't break a fragment
or lose what can't be lost.

i felt a silent reckoning on my body
i held a guitar in my hands
that would but be a way
to make me feel happy
playing its string of delusion on my head
voicing; *i might be healed.*

i am like an open book that is about to spell darkness in day
light
i will tell the sun everything i know
about the darkest curves on earth
i am on the wheel driving straight
to where i might see the sun shine
upon me
i have walked alone inside my house
so i might not die
but it's hard to believe something I'm not
that someday my body will open to the darkest curves

& perhaps,
when the sun shines.

2. mother says i shouldn't move out
that my body is highly sensitive to sunlight
that my body is a sepulcher

worshipping its own immune hypersensitive self
like bacteria that acuminate my body

& indeed
this is
a disorder
like the one who returns
hope with grief
gold with silver
but fate
befalling them all
like cone on my body
masochism makes the day
disturb the peace of raising
calls itself a monochrome of art
in my body
call it nausea of profundity
warped herself inside me
but do not call it grandeur
you can call what has rebel the fine babel of rhymes
a magnificent

some poems are like that;.
you call them beautiful
when their first sentence hasn't rescued
a depressed victim
hoping to pluck sweet fruit from a tree that lingers.

SCAR

your body
fire of a beast
the whole of you split
in two places
a scar
a scar
raised above me
covers my body
with woe
 yearned and
after, stained my skin
i yanked
as my body builds on a new scar
and what is found in my body
crossing and parting ways
create deep cuts
between dying and surviving.
a clatter of my mother's fetching tears
as she weeps and prays for my survival
of what is left in me

WHERE EVERYTHING ENDS IN ISOLATION

i am struck again by
social distancing
established in the heart
of many souls
this is what i call
vials of wrath
where everything ends
in hatred and agony
affliction and death
where languages
are symbols of litigation.
this time, my heart is wide open to embrace isolation